This book is dedicated to
Lylah and Violet Mouton.
Your curiosity is contagious.

In memory of Sotirios "Sotto" Vougiouklis.
Thank you for bringing this book to life.

A special thanks to our featured Tiny Thinker:
Violet Abell

CHARLIE
AND THE TORTOISE

Written by M.J. Mouton **Illustrated by Jezreel S. Cuevas**

A Foreword by Cara Santa Maria

Hi, I'm Cara! I love science. Science is a tool I use every day to learn more about the world around me. I've been doing science since I was just a little girl, when I dug holes in my backyard searching for dinosaur bones and caught lightning bugs in jars to see how they glow.

Charlie inspired me to follow my passions and to never stop asking questions. Eventually I grew up to become a scientist myself!

Now, I have the best job in the world. I get to go on TV and teach other people about science!

But I don't know everything about science. I still have lots of questions.

I like it when I don't know the answers to my questions, because then I can go on adventures to try to find them, just like Charlie!

I want to ask questions every single day.
I hope you do, too.

Will you join Hitch and me as we learn about Charlie's adventure?

Charlie loved being
outside with the
animals and plants.
With birds that tweet
and trees that dance.

Insects that crawl on you,
and frogs that jump away.
Oh, what else lies
far away?

He got his chance to sail the seas,
as he traveled from England to a faraway land,
to study the trees.
On a boat called the Beagle, he sailed.
What plants and animals would be unveiled?

The Beagle made many stops on the way,
and landed Charlie on an island one day.

It was just what he wished for
with animals, insects, and plants.
Turtles, and birds,
and lizards, and ants.

GALAPAGOS
N
CD

It was the Galapagos Islands,
and they are quite unique.
Thousands of different
species, so to speak.
Islands that people
had hardly ever seen,
vibrant and colorful,
with water so clean.

While Charlie watched
the different birds glide,
he studied them with a
tortoise at his side.

Charlie whipped out his book in a pinch,
and wrote, "This bird's beak is different,
but it's still a finch."

With not a single person in sight,
he leaned over to the tortoise and
asked "Am I right?"

The tortoise looked out of his shell just a peek,
looking at Charlie, too nervous to speak.

"I've noticed the birds.
I've been here a while...
for 200 years,"
he said with a smile.
"You'll have to bear with me.
I speak as slow as I walk."

To which Charlie exclaimed,
"Holy cow! You can talk!"
!!

"Some finches eat nuts, and some eat bugs.
Some eat grain, and some eat grubs."

"I think I know why their beaks made a change."

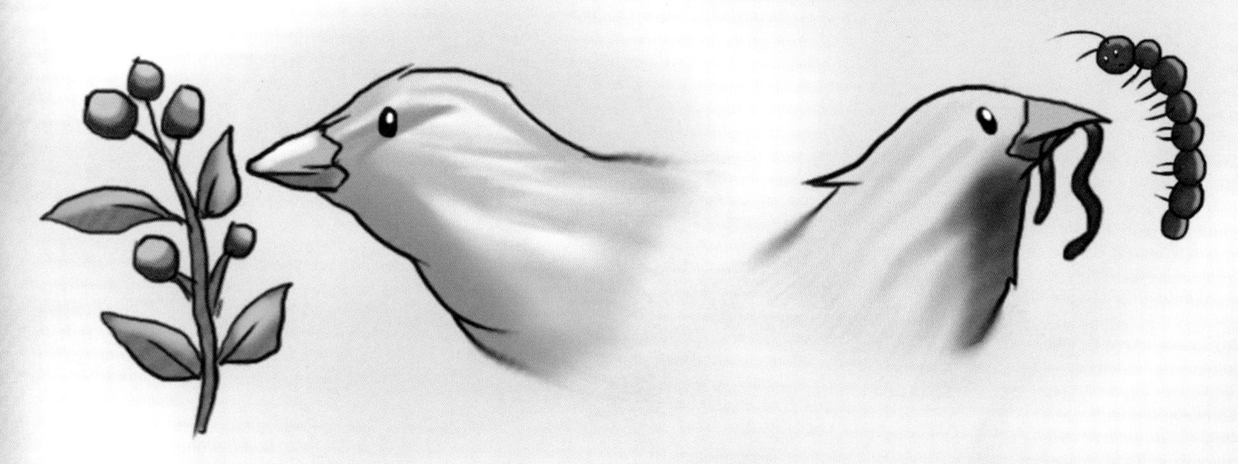

"They were on different islands,
with no food the same."

"Some finches have small beaks
that are pointed like spikes.
But a long time ago they
were once all alike."

"If the bird eats nuts, then his beak is much harder.
If it eats softer bugs, a softer beak is much smarter."

"Maybe this island
has bugs better at hiding,
so the birds eat the grains
they can get without trying."

"Or maybe the insects are smaller and faster.
So some birds' bodies may change to help them catch what they're after."

Charlie wrote it all down in
his nature book.
As the tortoise explained
how the finches look.

They spoke every day, as the tortoise imparted.
Until Charlie went back to the land he departed.

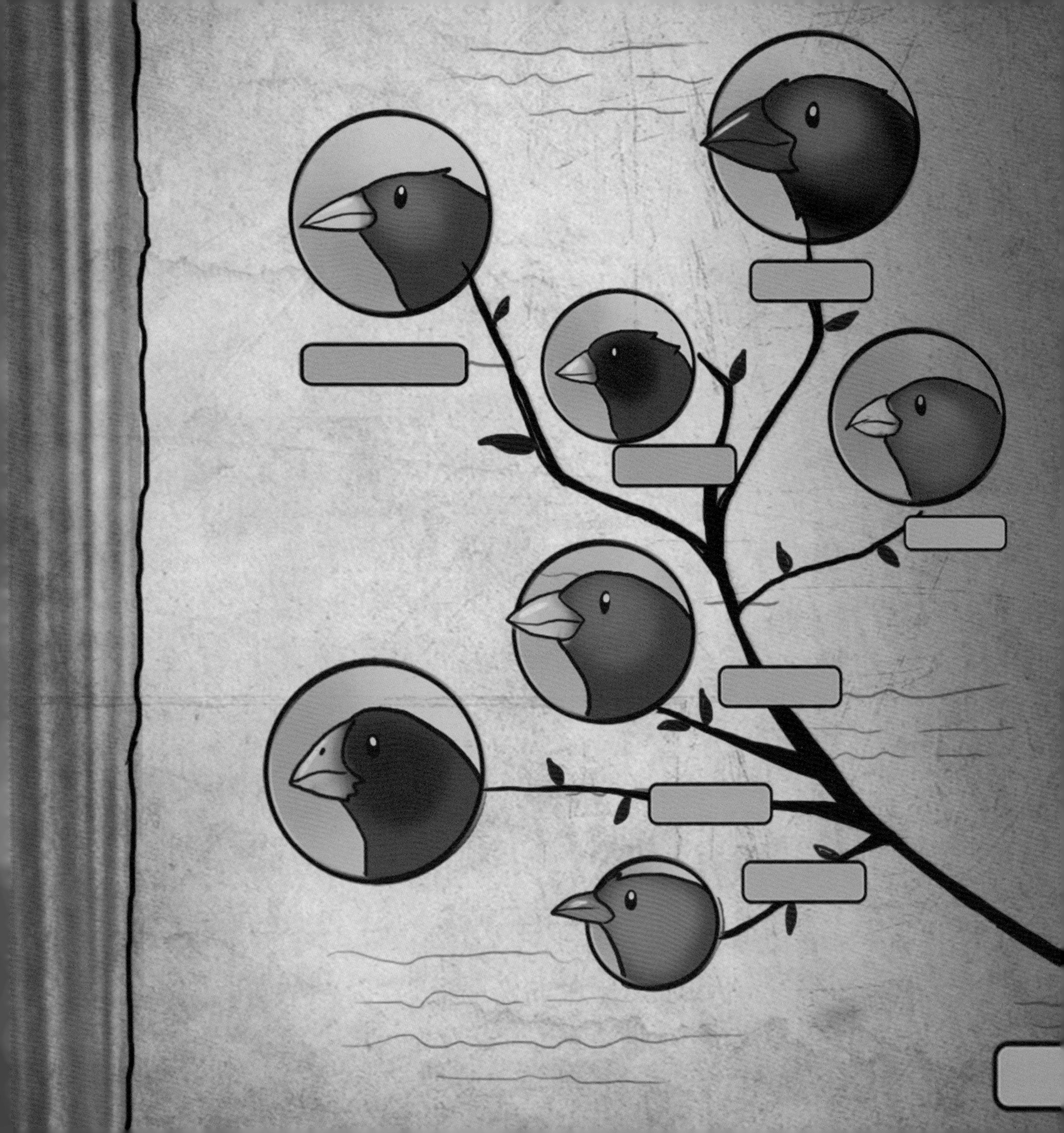

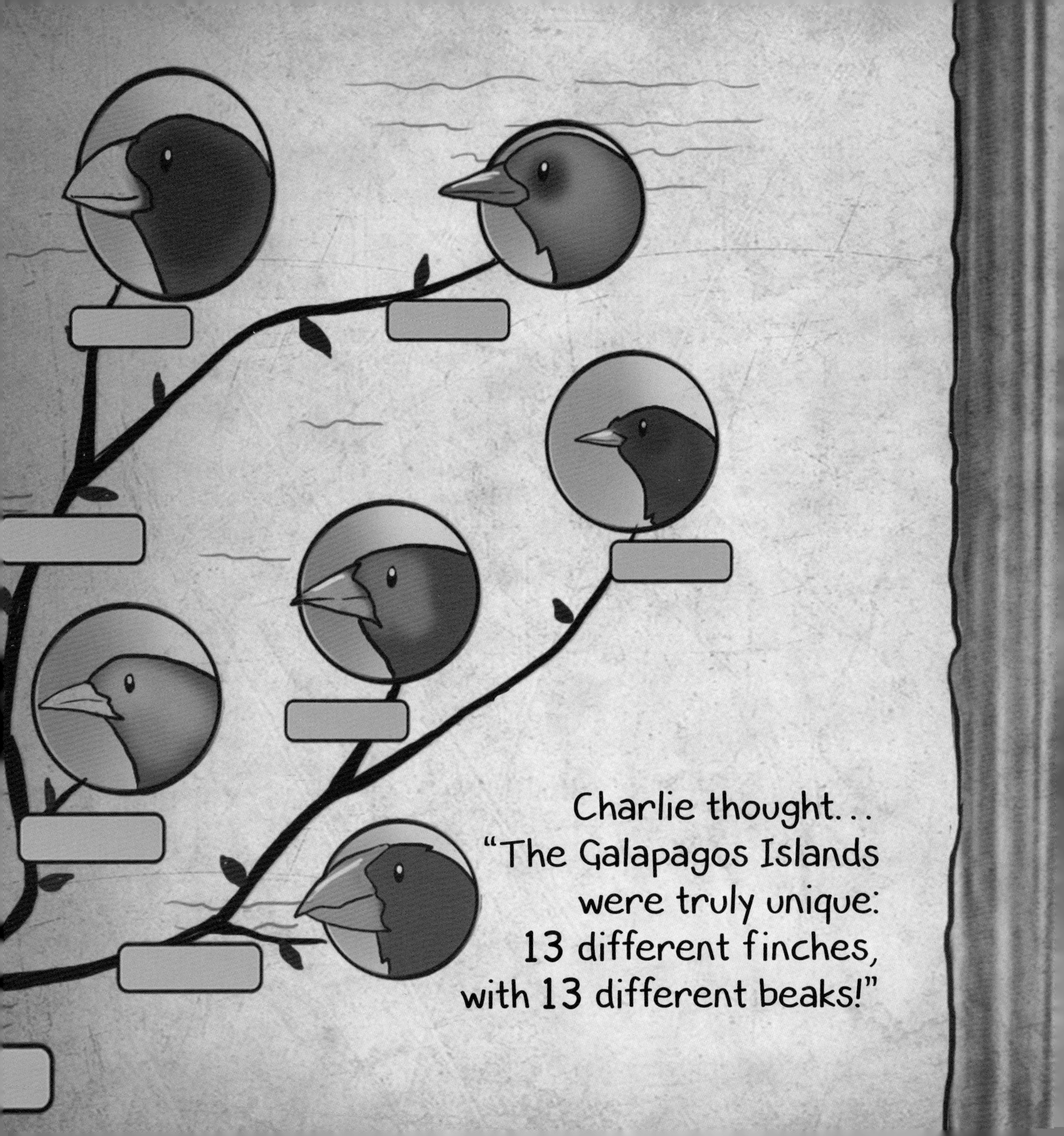
Charlie thought...
"The Galapagos Islands
were truly unique:
13 different finches,
with 13 different beaks!"

As Charlie got back to England,
he made a new book.
He wrote about small beaks,
large beaks, and beaks with a hook.

Charlie became quite famous for
what he discovered.
How animals change over time,
is what he uncovered!

After years of study,
Charlie taught the world,
that we're all connected,
every boy and every girl.

Every horse and every moose.
Every dog and every cat.
Every finch and every goose.
Even tortoises that chat!

THE END

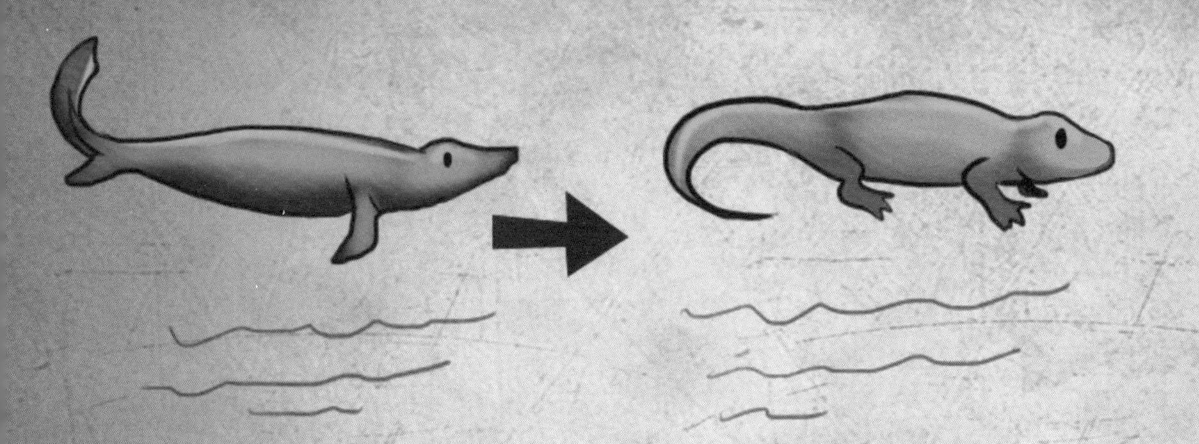

Charlie grew up to
be known as...

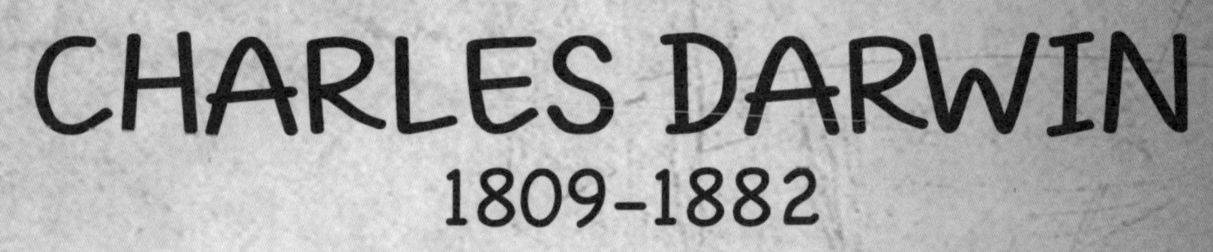
CHARLES DARWIN
1809-1882